D0125088

IS 61 LIBRARY

IS 61 LIBRARY

CLAUDIA AND THE NEW GIRL

Ann M. Martin

AN
APPLE
PAPERBACK

SCHOLASTIC INC.
New York Toronto London Auckland Sydney

*This book is for the loyal readers
of* The Baby-sitters Club *books.*

Cover art by Hodges Soileau

*If you purchased this book without a cover, you should be aware that this book
is stolen property. It was reported as "unsold and destroyed" to the publisher,
and neither the author nor the publisher has received any payment for this
"stripped book."*

No part of this publication may be reproduced in whole or in part,
or stored in a retrieval system, or transmitted in any form or by any
means, electronic, mechanical, photocopying, recording, or other-
wise, without written permission of the publisher. For information
regarding permission, write to Scholastic Inc., 555 Broadway, New
York, NY 10012.

ISBN 0-590-25167-8

Copyright © 1989 by Ann M. Martin. All rights reserved. Published
by Scholastic Inc. THE BABY-SITTERS CLUB, the BABY-SITTERS
CLUB logo, APPLE PAPERBACKS and the APPLE PAPERBACKS
logo are registered trademarks of Scholastic Inc.

12 11

0/0

Printed in the U.S.A.

40